Hello writing enthusiasts!

I'm not sure what inspired you to pick up this book. Maybe you want to practice writing. Maybe you're addicted to writing. Or, maybe someone gave it to you as a gift and now you're trying to figure out what to do with it.

I've always believed that writing was like any skill. It improves and becomes easier the more you do it. I hope you use this book to sharpen your skills.

A couple of things before you get started:

When you see references to "art", that could be a book, a film, a song, a painting, or any other form of art.

When you see the term "celebrity" it could be any famous person such as an actor, a politician, as serial killer…whatever inspires you.

If your real life doesn't fit a prompt, it's time to flex those fiction muscles.

Do the book in any order…front to back, jumping around, every other…just save the last one for last.

You can reach me at RitaBookBooks@gmail.com if you want to share your favorite stories or get on a mailing list as new books come out.

Have fun!!!

Sincerely, Rita

Write about a time you knew something was happening or had happened that was wrong, and you didn't say anything about it. If you could go back, would you do anything differently?

What is a piece of art that really stuck with you for days or weeks after you first experienced it? Why do you think it had that effect?

Think back to your 10-year-old self. Now write an accurate journal entry. What was going on in your life that your younger self would have written down?

____

____

____

____

____

____

____

____

____

____

____

____

____

____

____

____

____

____

Write about a time in your life when you were wrong. Really, really wrong. Not just a little wrong, like you pushed a door marked pull...but great big, "How could I have been so wrong?!?" wrong.

Earth is set for destruction by a race of alien beings pending a final visit to determine if it's worth saving. You have 24 hours to convince the visitors what makes Earth awesome, and humans worth saving. What do you show them?

What is the most underrated piece of art you know of? Why do you think it isn't appreciated by the masses?

You have woken up in unfamiliar woods. You have a phone that will only call one pre-programmed number. How do you explain your environment to the person on the other end of the line?

It turns out that a popular urban legend is based on something that really happened in your town, to the cousin of your best friend's next-door neighbor. But they didn't get the story quite right. What is the legend and the real story?

You are the author of a series of popular children's books written for kids 10 and under. What is your series about? What are your best-selling titles? Write at least 5-10 titles.

That thing in the back of the fridge you never threw out grew into a new life form. It has become a new pet. What did it start out as, and what did it turn into? What did you name it?

You are living off the grid for a year. You have no internet, and your electricity is limited to the hours of dusk to midnight. No trips into town. Necessities are delivered. How will you spend your days?

____

____

____

____

____

____

____

____

____

____

____

____

____

____

____

____

____

____

Have you lived in a variety of places or spent most of your life in the same place? What are the pros and cons? Does the grass look greener on the other side?

It's the first day of your new teaching job. What does your class look like? What are you teaching, and what part of the class will be the most surprising to your students?

Your life can easily be cut into two sections. Before this and after this. What is this?

It's remake time! It may or may not be your favorite movie, but this is a role you were born to play. It's the final audition. What's the movie, what's the part and what makes you so sure you're right for it?

____

____

____

____

____

____

____

____

____

____

____

____

____

____

____

____

You spent the last ten years time traveling. Now it's time for your press conference where you will show off your souvenirs and prove it to the world. What are we looking at?

____

____

____

____

____

____

____

____

____

____

____

____

____

____

____

____

____

____

____

What is a super practical thing nobody taught you that you had to learn on your own?

Somebody out there is feeling defeated and needs a boost. Tell them about an accomplishment of yours that surprised people, maybe even yourself.

You have been given a very accurate, but very limited psychic ability.
You can't predict things about death, money or love. Just this one
thing. What is it and how do you use your gift?

What is something you are constantly forgetting? Why do you think it is so hard for you to remember?

It was the best road trip ever! Just you and your favorite celebrity. Where did you go, and what was the best part of the trip?

What is a keepsake you have that a maid mistake for garbage and throw away? What makes it worth keeping for you?

This page is magical. What you write on this page no longer has power over you.

The app guarantees you a new group of awesome friends. You're meeting them for the first time around a campfire. Describe the group.

Forget about a better mousetrap! What we really need is a better......

What are the words you wish you could take back more than any other?

The house has been vacant for over 50 years. The trunk has been in the basement for at least that long. It took a lot of effort to open it. What is inside?

You've been dead 100 years, and someone is publishing your biography. Why are they writing about you? What is the title of the book and what does the cover look like?

A non-profit has been started in your honor. What is it called? What is its main purpose and why should society care?

Write about a stranger you still think of. How did you meet this person and why do you still think about them? What if you crossed paths with them again?

You were researching your family history and made a shocking discovery! Did anyone else in the family know about it or were they hearing about it for the first time?

Write about a time you should have said no.

Write about a time you should have said yes.

You travel back in time and find yourself as a child. You hand little you a notecard and say, "Keep this and look at it every day." What does the notecard say?

Now's the time. Pick a person and what it is that you need to say to them.

What was the first thing you ever saved up money to buy?

Who deserves a Thank You note? Write it here.

You wake up as a cartoon character. Who are you and what are you doing today?

You have just won a lifetime supply of _________. Most people don't really get why you're so excited, but you are thrilled. What is it and why are you so happy?

Think about an inanimate object in your home. Now write a story from its point of view.

____

____

____

____

____

____

____

____

____

____

____

____

____

____

____

____

____

____

You have been asked to write a sequel to your favorite book/movie that isn't part of a series. What story are you continuing, and what will happen?

You can "do-over" one thing in your life. Considering the "butterfly effect", what things in your life are now different?

Your online dating app has had no responses. You can't imagine why. Let's take a look at your profile.

Write about a time in your life when one door closed and another opened.

You've been thinking about it for a long time. People have tried to talk you out of it, but you're finally gonna do it. You're changing your name. What is your new name and how did you pick it?

____

____

____

____

____

____

____

____

____

____

____

____

____

____

____

____

____

I know these things to be true.

You are going on tour with your favorite singer/band. Describe the
tour.

____

____

____

____

____

____

____

____

____

____

____

____

____

____

____

____

____

____

____

What are the hard truths we have to accept in life?

Not trying to be weird or anything, but this fictional character could be my soulmate.

You wake up in the afterlife. Set the scene.

Required reading list for high school students. Be prepared to defend your selections.

Are you an accurate representation of your generation? How so? If not, what generation do you relate to the most?

Is there someone you thought you would share lifelong friendship with that isn't in your life anymore? What caused this? Can it be fixed? Do you want to fix it?

Time to put words in someone else's mouth. Who is the person and what do you need to hear them say?

____

____

____

____

____

____

____

____

____

____

____

____

____

____

____

____

____

____

____

You are designing your own tourist attraction. Where and what will it be (theme park, museum, tour)? Why will people come from all over to experience it?

It's time for your town's annual Proud of Our Town Parade. What does your float look like?

What are five things you currently own that you really should get rid of? You're never going to use them. (Extra credit if you actually get rid of them)

____

____

____

____

____

____

____

____

____

____

____

____

____

____

____

____

____

____

All you were trying to do was go for a walk, away from city noises, and enjoy a little nature. Nobody warned you to watch out for _________.

The building sits on the very edge of town. It's been abandoned for over 40 years. Today is the day you're going in. What do you know about it? What do you find inside?

____

____

____

____

____

____

____

____

____

____

____

____

____

____

____

____

____

It's been said that "Ignorance is Bliss". What's something you wish you didn't know?

Who is a teacher or boss that had a huge impact on your life? Do they know? Would you like to tell them?

This is your chance to save your favorite show from cancellation.
You have just been cast as a reoccurring character. What's the show
and how do you save it?

Find a historical event that happened the year you were born that surprised you.

____

____

____

____

____

____

____

____

____

____

____

____

____

____

____

____

____

____

____

You are home alone and sound asleep. There's a noise that wakes you up. It's not a big noisy, or particularly scary. But it does wake you up. When you go to investigate, what do you find?

You know you're going to catch heat for this, but you just find
___________ to be so overrated!

Friends with an ex….possible or impossible?

12 year-old finds a treasure map of the forest behind your house. Is this a solo mission or are you going with a group of friends? What happens?

It's time to give your Valedictorian speech (if you were Valedictorian, what would you go back and say knowing what you know now?).

There's something laying on the ground. It's nothing "important",
but you'll bet someone is missing it. What is it and who is missing it?

You can't believe it, but you just found out this song was written about you! What are we listening to?

What story would be more interesting if told from a different characters perspective (could be book, movie, TV)

You're your grandmother died she left you a box of old love letters from a historical figure. Who was in love with grandma, and why didn't it work out?

What is a little known event you would love to turn into a
book/film?

Who is a villain you just can't help but root for?

The ultimate "walk a mile in someone else's shoes"…if you could make someone (or a type of someone) wake up in someone else's body and live their life for a week what scenario would you create?

Write a short story about yourself that starts with the sentence, "Well, I finally did it."

It turns out the house you bought is home to the ghost of a very famous historical figure. Who are you hanging out with?

There is a mirror in the attic, but it doesn't just show your reflection.
It shows you something else. What can you see?

You've been invited to compete on a reality show. You know you are going to win. What is the concept of the show? Don't use an existing reality show.

What is something you used to be certain of that you have since
changed your mind about?

You had a dream that was so real, you know it's going to come true.
No one will believe you. What was the dream?

Describe a major event and trace it back to the seemingly insignificant decision or event that led to it.

Two people are cleaning up after a party and find something that reveals something shocking about one of the guests. What did they find and what's the shocking news?

A little boy wanders away at a carnival and ends up lost inside a fun house. Write about his experience.

Write about a character coming out of a 50-year sleep. When did they go to sleep and what are they waking up to?

Your cousin shows up to Thanksgiving with the new person they're dating, and it turns out it's someone you used to date. Describe dinner.

Write about a major historical event seen through the eyes of a child
(But not a historical event you witnessed as a child)

It could have been so good, but they ruined it with the ending. Re-
write the ending!

Describe a convention for a hobby/interest that most people have never heard of. How would people dress up? What would the panels be like?

You're skating on a frozen pond and see something under the ice that shouldn't be there. What is it? How do you think it got there and are you going to try to get it out?

There's something you used to love to do when you were younger. One day you did it for the last time. What was it? What if you could do it again?

Write a short story told only with dialogue.

Write a story that starts with someone making a promise they know they will not keep and then describe how they break that promise.

Write about someone who gets several amazing offers in the same day, but by accepting one they have to turn down the others.

Write about a character who has to do something completely outside their comfort zone in order to collect an amazing inheritance.

Write about someone trying to atone for something they'll never really be able to make up for.

A young priest goes to hear a deathbed confession. He hears something unexpected. What is it?

Pretty in Pink or Pretty Woman? Defend your decision.

They're making a TV show based on your life. Who's going to play you? What will you use for the theme song?

____

____

____

____

____

____

____

____

____

____

____

____

____

____

____

____

____

____

Look back over the rest of the book. Is there anything you wrote that you want to expand on, or have you been inspired to write something else?

9 798450 853499